# COSMIC CREATURES
### A whole new world of animal rescue!

## The **Snuggly Snowpop**

**ILLUSTRATED BY**
**SOPHY**
**WILLIAMS**

## TOM HUDDLESTON

nosy
crow

First published in the UK in 2022 by Nosy Crow Ltd
The Crow's Nest, 14 Baden Place
Crosby Row, London, SE1 1YW, UK

Nosy Crow Eireann Ltd
44 Orchard Grove, Kenmare,
Co Kerry, V93 FY22, Ireland

Nosy Crow and associated logos are trademarks and/or
registered trademarks of Nosy Crow Ltd

Text copyright © Tom Huddleston, 2022
Illustrations © Sophy Williams, 2022

ISBN: 978 1 83994 133 7

A CIP catalogue record for this book will be available from the British Library

Printed and bound in Great Britain by Clays Ltd, Elcograf S.p.A.

Papers used by Nosy Crow are made from wood grown in sustainable forests.

MIX
Paper from
responsible sources
FSC® C018072

1 3 5 7 9 10 8 6 4 2

www.nosycrow.com

## Chapter One
# Base Camp

Charlie stepped from the tent, wrapped her woolly coat around her and shivered. The mountain air was bitterly cold. In the sky, the two suns of planet Vela were setting behind the mountains, casting long blue shadows across the face of the glacier.

"Come on, Random," Charlie called. "Before we freeze solid!"

Random the robot floated out, zipped

the tent and secured its heat-seal. He
bobbed beside Charlie as they started
uphill. Snow crunched beneath Charlie's
padded boots as they passed the huddle
of canvas tents that Captain Robertson
had named Base Camp. Above them rose
a nameless peak – the highest mountain
on Vela.

"I wonder if we'll be able to climb it
tomorrow," Charlie said.

Random peered into the sky. "It will
depend on the weather," he said. "We
need a clear day if the captain wants to
make his attempt on the summit."

"I still don't understand why he's so
keen to be the first one to climb it," said
Charlie. "Why doesn't he just fly up
there?"

Charlie's family and their fellow settlers
had travelled from Earth to study Vela,
and to live in harmony with its incredible

plants and animals. She didn't see what trudging all the way up a massive mountain had to do with any of that.

There was a sudden humming behind them. It grew louder until, without warning, a flurry of powdery snow covered Charlie and Random.

Charlie groaned. "Hello, Miranda," she said, as the girl skidded to a halt and kicked snow off her power-skis.

Miranda removed a pair of infrared goggles and tugged off her super-heated gloves. "Evening," she smirked. "What have you two been up to? Something thrillingly exciting, no doubt."

Charlie felt herself blush. She didn't want to admit that she and Random had been sitting in their tent playing cards for the past hour while they waited for dinner.

She knew the captain's daughter from school, but they'd never been friends. Miranda seemed to prefer the company of her father to that of her classmates. This was the first time they'd spent any time together – and Charlie was already hoping it would be the last.

Miranda laughed. "Honestly, you should get yourself some of these power-skis. They're so much fun. Oh, wait, I forgot, this is the only pair on Vela. Bye!"

She squeezed the control pad and the skis powered up, carrying her away across the snow.

Charlie grimaced. "Just because she's got those fancy skis and goggles and everything, she thinks she's so much better than everyone else."

Random let out an electronic sigh. "She is only human," he said.

Charlie looked up as a beam of light slanted across the snowy ground. It was coming from a large tent just up ahead. The flap had opened to allow Miranda inside and Charlie saw her father in the doorway, beckoning as he spotted her.

"Come along," he called out. "Dinner's getting cold."

Charlie hurried up the slope and pushed into the tent with Random right behind her. Her father, Kwame, secured the heat-seal and Charlie felt her cheeks flush in the sudden warmth.

In the centre of the tent was a table laid for dinner. Captain Robertson sat at the head with a mug of steaming tea. He was a big man with a black moustache and a very loud voice. He'd piloted the ship that had brought the settlers to Vela, and when they landed he'd nominated himself as their leader. It was two years since he'd flown the ship but he still wore a captain's badge on his lapel.

Miranda took a seat, looking up at her father adoringly. Two young settlers entered from the adjoining kitchen. Their names were Hiroshi and Chiara, and they'd been helping the captain plan for the big climb. They placed a platter of freshly made bread and a steaming pan of stew on the table, and everyone tucked in.

"So, weatherman," the captain said, fixing Kwame with a piercing stare. "Do you think it'll be safe to climb tomorrow?"

# Cosmic Creatures

Charlie's father frowned, then he nodded. "The forecast's looking good," he said. "But remember, the weather on Vela can be extremely unpredictable. That's what you get when you have five moons and two suns."

"But we also have you," said the captain. "The best meteorologist on the planet."

Charlie smiled at her dad. Kwame did know a lot about the weather. It was what made him such a good farmer, and it was also why the captain had asked him to come along on this expedition.

"I can't wait," Miranda piped up excitedly. "You're going to be the first person to climb the highest mountain on the whole planet. And I'm going to be the second."

"That's the spirit," the captain beamed. "Tomorrow I will plant my flag and

name the peak Mount Robertson. And
you will be right by my—"

"Hush!" Random said suddenly, and
the captain looked at him in annoyance.

"My apologies," the robot whispered.
"But my sensors are picking up
movement outside the tent. And we are
all here."

They listened intently, but all Charlie
could hear was the wind.

"There's nothing out there," Miranda
muttered loudly to her father. "That old
robot has got his circuits crossed. He
probably—"

There was a cry, louder than the wind,
right outside the tent. Miranda clamped
a hand over her mouth and the captain
jumped to his feet. He tugged on his coat
and hurried to the door. Kwame and the
other settlers were right behind him.

The captain flung open the tent flap

and marched out into the snow. Beyond him, Charlie saw a shadowy shape ducking behind one of the tents. Past it, she saw another moving figure, and another, barely visible in the moonlight.

"Animals!" the captain cried. "They must be after our supplies."

He tugged something from his belt and raised it in the air. There was a deafening bang and Base Camp was suddenly flooded with red light as the captain released a flare into the sky. It arced upwards like a firework.

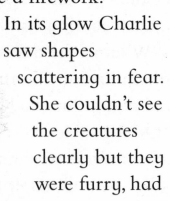

In its glow Charlie saw shapes scattering in fear. She couldn't see the creatures clearly but they were furry, had two legs and seemed about half her height. They scampered over the snow on big fluffy feet.

"Did you really need to scare them like that?" she asked, as the captain lowered his flare pistol.

"They were here to steal our food," he snapped, and marched back to the tent. He stopped in the doorway, pointing a finger at Charlie. "You're too soft-hearted, that's your problem."

Then he turned and Charlie saw his mouth drop open. From inside she heard a clattering and screeching and saw lights flickering wildly.

"What in the galaxy..." the captain said in horror. Charlie peered past him, and almost laughed out loud.

On the table was one of the creatures, only this one was much smaller – just a baby, she realised. It had bright-blue eyes and bushy white fur with silvery zigzag stripes. It was crouching by the pot of stew, shoving fistfuls into its mouth and chattering excitedly.

Above the table, a lantern hung from a long electrical cord. Another of the creatures gripped the cable in its tiny hands, swinging back and forth and giggling wildly. This one's pelt was pure white, and it had tufty ears that stuck up from its head.

The captain rushed into the tent, waving his arms.

"Shoo!" he shouted. "Begone, beasties!"

The creature on the table sprang up, scattering forks and plates and splattering stew everywhere. The other creature clambered up the lantern cord and hung from the ceiling, squeaking excitedly.

"Hello there," Charlie said, peering up at it. "Don't worry, we won't hurt you."

"Maybe not," the captain growled.
"But we will see you off. Shoo!"

He moved round the table, trying to
chase the first creature back towards
the door. But just then Random came
floating in and the little animal squeaked

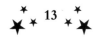

in surprise, jumping on to a counter and sending maps and geographical documents flying. Charlie couldn't help laughing. The captain scowled at her.

"Don't just stand there," he said. "Do something!"

"Like what?" Charlie asked.

"I don't know," the captain snarled. "Aren't you supposed to be good with animals?"

The tufty-eared creature dropped from the ceiling, landing on the tent floor. It grabbed a discarded boot and started gnawing on it. Its stripy companion seized the boot as well and they wrestled for control, squeaking and play-fighting. The scene reminded Charlie of her little brother, Maki, who was back in First Landing with their mum.

"I think they must be family," Charlie said. "But I've never seen anything like them before. I don't know if anyone has."

The two creatures settled down, each of them chewing on one end of the boot. Then suddenly a cry cut through the air and they looked up, ears standing on end. They glanced at one another as the cry came again, a ghostly howling in the dark.

Then they dropped the boot and scampered to the door, hurrying beneath Random and between the startled settlers. Miranda squealed in surprise as the little creatures darted past her and vanished into the night to join their pack.

## Chapter Two
# The Climb

The next morning dawned bright and clear. The captain was up with the suns, marching through Base Camp, shouting for everyone to rise and shine. Charlie rolled over in her bunk and groaned, but she knew she didn't have a choice.

Her father came in with a mug of hot cocoa just as she was pulling on her third layer of warm clothes.

"Drink this," Kwame said. "Then follow

me. He's in no mood to wait."

The captain stood outside the big tent, tapping his foot impatiently. Miranda smirked at Charlie, snug inside her heated jacket.

"About time," the captain snapped. "So, are we safe to climb?"

Kwame nodded. "I think so. There's a storm front gathering to the west, but it shouldn't arrive until tomorrow."

The captain waved a dismissive hand. "By then we'll be packed up and on our way home," he said. "Nothing to worry about."

"You're probably right," Kwame agreed, "but listen. If that storm moves faster than expected, or if anything else goes wrong, I want you to promise we'll come down. I won't risk Charlie's safety on this expedition, all right?"

The captain's face reddened. He wasn't

used to being spoken to like that. But he nodded briskly. "I didn't ask you to bring the child along, but of course her safety and that of my own daughter are of primary importance."

They set off, marching up the steep slope towards the peak. The captain took the lead, followed by Miranda on her power-skis. Charlie trudged behind with Random, and Kwame brought up the rear. Chiara and Hiroshi remained behind to guard the camp in case the furry creatures returned.

"It's best to make the final ascent with as small a group as possible," the captain explained as they walked. "Much smaller risk of accidents, you see."

"So what's *she* doing here?" Miranda muttered, glancing back at Charlie. But either the captain didn't hear or he didn't care to reply.

The sun was high by the time they reached the top of the first slope. Beyond it was a wide, shallow valley – a great blue ice field that shimmered beneath the sky. Charlie took a break by leaning on Random, his floating body holding her up. Her friend didn't mind. He never got tired.

They followed the ridge for a while, scrambling over shingle and rockslides, stepping in the shadows of boulders that must have been there for thousands of years. Miranda had removed her power-skis and now she puffed and panted along the path ahead of Charlie, hurrying to keep up with her father. But the captain didn't look back, he just kept his eyes fixed on the peak rising above them.

Soon they began to descend, tramping down into the valley. Ahead of them, Charlie could see a line of shadow, and as they drew closer she realised it was a grove of large plants.

They were as tall as trees, but they were quite unlike any other plants Charlie had ever seen. Their bark was smooth and shiny, and their long branches held no leaves, only waving fronds like the gills on a star-newt. Beneath their boughs the ground was clear of snow, mottled with moss and lichen. In the hush, Charlie heard the chittering of small birds, and saw tiny, furred creatures scurrying into their burrows.

"Remarkable," Kwame said, inspecting the plants. "Touch the bark, it's warm."

Charlie stroked the tree. Her father was right, there was a gentle warmth there. No wonder this grove was so popular with birds and animals, she thought – it must make a cosy shelter among the hard rocks and biting wind.

"We're not here to study botany," the captain growled. "You can come back and do that in your own time. According to my satellite scans, just beyond this grove will be the trickiest part of the climb. So let's keep moving."

He was soon proved right. As they emerged from the grove they saw a cliff rising ahead of them, made entirely of ice. The captain took out an ice axe and unwound a rope from his pack.

"This looks tricky," Kwame said. "Isn't there another way round?"

"There is, but it's too slow," the captain said. "This is a shortcut. Straight up the face of this glacier, then we're almost at the peak."

"I could use my force field to carry the girls to the top," Random offered. "Then we could throw down a rope for the two of you."

The robot often extended his force field around Charlie to carry her along, but she knew he wasn't powerful enough to lift larger objects like the two men.

Miranda snorted in horror. "I wouldn't trust that rickety old robot to take me anywhere," she said. "Besides, we're here to climb this mountain, not be carried up it."

The captain smiled. "That's my girl. Now, just step where I step and you'll be fine."

He used his ice axe to chip a hole in the face of the cliff, then he tapped in a small metal spike called a piton and used that to climb higher. He dropped a rope and Miranda tied herself on. Then she began to climb after him.

Charlie beckoned to Random. "I'll climb too. But keep an eye on Miranda. If she gets in trouble, she might need your help."

"Very well," the robot said softly. "But I'll

be watching you as well."

Charlie was an experienced climber. She'd had plenty of practice in the trees and caves around First Landing. But she was glad to have Random humming beside her as she hauled herself up the wall of ice. The surface was smooth like glass, and although it was rock-hard, she knew there was always a risk it could chip and shatter.

As she climbed, she noticed something strange. There was a hole in the ice just off to her left, a circular opening like the mouth of a tunnel. As she peered closer she was sure she saw movement inside, just for a moment.

"Keep up," Miranda called over her shoulder. "Honestly, I heard you were some sort of expert climber."

Charlie scowled and tightened her grip. She knew she shouldn't let Miranda's words get to her, but she couldn't help it.

Looking down, she saw her father scaling the rope. Beyond him was a long, straight drop to the valley floor. They'd already climbed a good distance. She wondered how much further there was to go.

"I should've let you carry me," she muttered to Random as the robot drifted higher. "Honestly, this is all just a lot of—"

She broke off. Just above and to the left was another one of those strange holes in the ice. There was a sound coming from it – a faint, friendly chattering, almost like laughter.

Miranda narrowed her eyes. "Was that you?" she asked.

Charlie shook her head. "It came from in there," she said. "Wait, be careful!"

But it was too late. Miranda had pulled herself to the opening, using the rope to swing across. She grabbed on and peered inside.

Then with a shriek she kicked away from the cliff.

Inside the opening Charlie saw a furry white face. It squeaked as Miranda toppled back, let go of the rope and began to fall.

# Chapter Three

# The Long Way

Random swooped in, extending his force field around Miranda. She came to a sudden stop, tumbling in mid-air with a startled expression. Two furry faces peeped from the opening in the ice, chattering to one another.

"What's going on?" the captain called down. "Miranda, are you hurt?"

Miranda managed to roll over so she was facing up towards her father. "They just startled me," she said. "The little beasts came out of nowhere."

*I tried to warn you*, Charlie thought, but she didn't say it. The creatures peered at Miranda as she hung suspended below them.

"It's lucky Random was there," Kwame said. "He just saved your life."

"It was my pleasure," the robot said. "Now, would you like me to—"

*Clunk!*

Random looked up. "What's happening?"

Charlie almost laughed. The robot appeared to have grown a furry wig, covering the top of his shiny metal head.

The stripy creature had leapt from the hole in the ice and landed on Random. It gripped the aerial that sprouted from the centre of the robot's head. Random rolled around and the creature squealed as he rocked from side to side.

"Be careful!" Charlie said. "Don't tip him off."

The tufty-eared creature followed his brother from the opening, but he didn't jump on Random. Instead, he took hold of the rope, clinging to it like a monkey on a vine. He bobbed up and down and the captain looked down in annoyance.

"What is going on?" he demanded.

"It's those little monsters," Miranda shouted. "They're ruining everything."

"They're just having fun," Charlie said. "They think we're playing a game."

The tufty-eared creature slid down the rope towards her, dropping until he and Charlie were almost face to face. "Hello again," she said. "Are you enjoying yourself?"

The creature let out a happy squeal and the captain glowered.

"I'm coming down," he said. "I'll deal with these fiends."

He set off, using the pitons to climb down. But he was angry and careless, putting too much weight on the little metal spikes. Charlie heard a deep creaking noise, following by a splitting crack.

Kwame's eyes widened. "Be careful!" he

cried out. "The ice is breaking!"

But it was too late. The captain tried to swing clear but his weight on one of the pitons had split the cliff. Something slid past Charlie's face. It was a shard of ice as long as her arm. It was soon followed by another.

Kwame beckoned urgently. "Charlie, quick, climb down to me," he shouted. "Random, get Miranda to safety!"

Random floated away from the cliff, carrying Miranda with him. Charlie started to climb down, but then she saw both creatures clinging to the rope above her head. They looked terrified as the cliff cracked and slivers of ice came tumbling past.

"Come on," Charlie said, holding up her arm. "I'll protect you."

The striped creature jumped on to her shoulder and the tufty-eared one joined him, clinging to Charlie's ear. Above her,

# CosmIC Creatures

Charlie could see the captain dropping rapidly, the rope sliding through his hands.

"Move!" he barked, so she did, using the wall of the cliff to keep her balance. The ground rushed up towards her and she felt her father's hands pulling her in. Great chunks of ice came crashing and smashing around them.

Charlie unclipped from the rope and ran with Kwame to the shelter of the trees. The captain was right behind them.

As they reached the forest there was a deafening crash, and a cloud of ice-splinters swept over them. Charlie felt the little creatures trembling as they clung on.

Gradually, the cloud cleared and the din died away. Random floated down, carrying Miranda with him. She looked scared but relieved. Charlie took a breath, mopping the melting ice from her hair and her face.

"Well," Kwame said bitterly. "So much for your shortcut."

At the foot of the cliff was a huge pile of frozen debris and loose shards. The cliff itself was a wreck: a jagged patchwork of cracked ice. There was no way to climb it; at least, not safely.

"Once again, I offer my services," Random said. "I could carry Charlie up and—"

"No!" the captain snapped. "I came to test myself against this mighty peak and I intend to do so. It may have won this round but I'm not beaten yet!"

Miranda's face glowed with admiration. "That's right, Dad," she said. "Let's show this stupid mountain who's boss."

"So we have to take the long way round?" Charlie asked.

The captain nodded. "We may not get back to Base Camp until nightfall. But I don't think we have any choice."

"Don't forget the storm," Kwame warned. "We mustn't risk getting caught in it."

"You said it wouldn't be here until tomorrow," the captain snapped. He marched off through the forest of plants. "Come on!"

"Um, what about these two?" Charlie asked, gesturing to the furry creatures who crouched on her shoulders. "Shall I bring them with us?"

The captain turned. His eyebrows shot up.

"Most certainly not!" he said. "They've caused enough trouble for one day. You will leave them here. That is an order. No doubt they'll find their way back to their nest, or their burrow, or whatever infernal hole they crawled out of."

## Chapter Four
# Unwanted Guests

Charlie placed the creatures on a patch of dry ground and gave each of them a pat on the head.

"Maybe I'll see you again on the way down," she told them, then she set off after the others.

The captain set a brisk pace, following the base of the cliff. The valley sloped upwards and they struggled on, through deep snowdrifts and fields of fallen boulders.

At first Miranda marched right behind her father but soon she began to fall behind, unable to keep the pace.

"Why don't you clip on your skis?" Charlie asked as she caught up to her.

Miranda scowled. "You heard my father. That would be cheating."

Charlie decided not to point out that Miranda had used them at the start of the journey. Instead, she gritted her teeth and kept marching.

The captain paused in the shadow of a big rock and took out his water bottle. Suddenly he jumped back. "You again!"

The two creatures lay on their backs on the rock, sunning themselves. They jumped up happily as Charlie gave them a wave.

"How did you get here so fast?" she asked.

"Don't encourage them!" the captain

snapped. "Tell them to go away."

"I don't think they'll listen," Charlie said. "Sorry."

The creatures followed them for the next hour, bounding over the snow on their flat, furry feet. They climbed on rocks and dangled from icicles, rolled in the snow and popped up unexpectedly from hidden burrows.

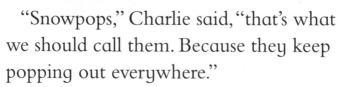

"Snowpops," Charlie said, "that's what we should call them. Because they keep popping out everywhere."

"It's perfect," Miranda grumbled. "A silly name for a silly little creature."

Charlie ignored the comment. "I'll name the silvery one Zig-Zag, because of the stripes on his tummy," she decided. "And the white one I'll call Tufty, for his ears."

Miranda rolled her eyes. "Call them whatever you like," she said, and strode after her father.

After a long march they reached another ridge, and now they could see the summit of the mountain rising high on their right. It was further than Charlie had expected, its peak wreathed in cloud.

"That isn't good," Kwame said, and the captain turned on him.

"What?" he frowned. "What's the problem now?"

"It's too far," said Kwame. "We're still a long way from the top and it's past midday."

"Then we need to pick up the pace," the captain said.

"That's not—" Kwame began, then he broke off, glancing at Miranda. "That's not possible. If it was just you and me, then perhaps, but..."

Realisation dawned on the captain's face. "I see," he said. "Yes, I see your point. These girls are slowing us down."

Charlie opened her mouth to protest, but Kwame gave her a stern look.

Miranda stared at her father in horror. For a moment she couldn't even speak, then she clasped her hands together pleadingly.

"I can go faster," she said. "Dad, I can, I just—"

The captain shook his head. "Kwame's right. I know you mean well, but the simple fact is that your stride isn't as long as ours, and you're not as experienced at climbing. That'll become a problem as we get closer to the top."

"It's my fault too," Charlie said. "I'm going as fast as I can. I suppose it's just not fast enough." Kwame reached for her hand and squeezed it gratefully.

"So what can we do?" Miranda asked, wiping her eye angrily with the corner of her sleeve. "Just give up?"

"No," the captain said. "But we shall have to leave you girls behind. You can shelter by these rocks until we return."

"They should go back to camp," Kwame said. "Just in case that storm hits."

"No!" Miranda protested. "No, I refuse,

I won't, I—"

The captain put a hand on her arm, guiding her away and talking to her quietly.

Kwame smiled at Charlie. "Thanks for saying that," he said softly. "The only way she'll listen is if she thinks you're being sent back too. And you know the way to Base Camp, right?"

"Of course," Charlie said. "South-east to the forest, then south out of the valley."

Kwame nodded proudly. "Good. And, of course, Random will be with you, if anything goes wrong."

Charlie frowned. "Actually, I was thinking he should go with you. We'll be walking a path we already know. You'll be doing some difficult climbing. I doubt the captain will be as careful as he ought to be."

Kwame thought about this. Then he

looked at Random.

"What do you think, old friend? Fancy a trip to the top?"

The robot hummed. "If Charlie would like me to accompany you, then I'll gladly do so," he agreed. "Besides, I'd like to see Vela from its highest peak."

Charlie smiled. "Thanks, Random."

The captain didn't look very pleased when Kwame told him the robot was coming along, but he didn't argue. He shouldered his pack, ready to march.

"We won't be far behind you," he said to Miranda, who stood looking away at the distant horizon. "We'll make good time to the peak, then we'll head back down at double speed."

His daughter didn't turn around. "We were meant to go together," she muttered. "We were going to be first."

"I know, Miranda," the captain said

apologetically. "I'm sorry."

Charlie couldn't help thinking that if he was really sorry, he'd come back and try another day. But she knew that wasn't going to happen.

The two men set off along the ridge, with Random bobbing along behind them. Miranda watched until they vanished behind a fall of boulders, then she started downhill. Her boots crunched in the snow and her fists swung at her sides.

Charlie glanced at Zig-Zag, who crouched on a rock nearby.

"She'll get over it," Charlie said. "She can't stay in a bad mood forever."

But after an hour of downhill walking,

Miranda was still furious. She kicked her feet, sending up showers of grit and snow. And if one of the snowpops got too close, she snapped at them to leave her alone.

Avoiding Miranda, Zig-Zag and Tufty stayed with Charlie, riding on her shoulders or bounding across the rocks beside her. They seemed to enjoy play-fighting most of all, and she'd often look round to see them tumbling in the snow, giggling happily.

"You daft things," Charlie smiled. "I wonder where your home is."

Below them she could see the dark shadow of the forest. She thought it would take an hour to reach it. Then all they had to do was cross the valley, climb the ridge and descend to Base Camp on the far side. They'd be back long before dark.

Then she saw something beyond the ridge, and her heart began to beat a little faster. There was a shadow out there, carried on the wind. The surrounding mountains had stood out clear and crisp before, but now their outlines were growing hazy.

"Hang on," she called to Miranda. "Look at that."

She caught up to her, pointing towards the horizon.

"It's getting darker," Charlie said.

"So what?" Miranda asked.

"So it's still the middle of the day," Charlie pointed out. "And look, it's getting closer. A minute ago I could see a mountain peak over there. Now it's gone."

"It's just clouds," Miranda said.

"But what if it's not?" Charlie asked. "What if it's that storm?"

Miranda laughed. "You're just like your dad. Always worrying about nothing."

Charlie felt her cheeks redden. "Well, you're just like your dad," she said. "You never listen to anyone else."

Miranda scowled. "My father is a great man. He'll climb that mountain, just you wait."

"I'm sure he will, with my dad's help," Charlie said. "I just hope they can make it safely down again."

Charlie took her mini-com out of her

pocket, activating the little hand-held communicator. "Random," she said into it. "Random, can you hear me?"

For a moment there was silence, then a crackly voice came on.

"Charlie? Are ... all right?"

"We're fine," Charlie said. "I just wanted to warn you. I think that storm might be coming."

"Charlie?" Random said again. "You're breaking ... could hear was ... interference from... "

There was another hiss, then the signal cut out altogether. Charlie tried to peer up towards the peak, but she could see nothing but snow and cloud.

Then she turned to look down, and her pulse quickened. The shadow was even closer now, almost reaching the ridge.

"I'm sure it's the storm," she said, "and if we're not careful, we're going to be caught in it."

Miranda started to look worried. "But we can't possibly reach Base Camp," she said. "It's too far."

"What about your skis?" Charlie asked.

Miranda's face lit up. She unhooked the skis from her backpack. "You'll have to hang on to me," she said as she clipped them to her feet.

Charlie beckoned to Zig-Zag and Tufty, extending a hand for them to clamber up. She unzipped her coat and Zig-Zag snuggled down into it, but there was barely any room left for Tufty.

"Can you take him?" Charlie asked Miranda, gesturing to the little creature.

She scowled. "I'm going to be busy enough steering my skis," she said. "I don't have time to worry about some silly little beast."

Sighing, Charlie shuffled Zig-Zag over,

making just enough space for Tufty to fit. Their heads peeked over the top of her collar, their fur tickling her chin.

She stepped on to the skis behind Miranda, wrapping her arms around her waist. "Even if we can't reach Base Camp," she said, "if we can get to the forest, we can take shelter and figure out our next move."

Miranda squeezed the control panel and Charlie heard the power-skis hum. Then she thumbed the control stick forward and they were off.

## Chapter Five
# The Storm

The wind stung Charlie's cheeks as they
raced downhill. Miranda steered expertly,
weaving around rocks and boulders,
curving gracefully down the mountainside.

The little snowpops peeped from
Charlie's jacket, their ears pressed flat by
the rushing wind. The sky was darkening
and Charlie could feel the gusts growing
stronger. The forest was still some distance
away.

"We're not going to make it," she shouted over the howling gale. "Can't these things go any faster?"

"We're at top speed," Miranda called back. "But you can take over if you think you can do better."

"No, you're doing great," Charlie said. "I just—"

Without warning, the storm struck. Biting snow lashed at them and the wind was so powerful that Charlie and Miranda were almost knocked off the skis. The snowpops squeaked and hid themselves deep in Charlie's coat.

But Miranda angled the skis sideways, cutting across the wind like a ship tacking on the ocean. They kept their balance, crouching as low as they could.

The world around them vanished. Charlie could barely see her own hands through the clouds of swirling snow.

"How will we find the forest?" she cried.

Miranda held up her control panel. "Before we started, I pointed this at the forest and it memorised the direction,' she called. "It will keep the skis on the right course."

A dark shape rose up ahead and Miranda moved the stick, steering them past a tall, craggy boulder. Then Charlie felt the skis turning, guiding them back downhill.

"That's really clever," she said. "Now we just have to hope we don't freeze."

She was glad of the little snowpops nestled in her coat, warm against her chest. She clutched Miranda tightly as they sped into the heart of the storm.

It wasn't long before she saw more shadows ahead. But these weren't rocks – they were too oddly shaped. Soon the wind dropped and Charlie saw pale-grey branches arching overhead.

Miranda slowed the skis and Charlie hopped off, landing on soft mossy soil. The snowpops jumped out of her coat, scampered over to one of the trees and wrapped their arms around its trunk.

"Of course!" Charlie remembered. "The trees are warm."

She copied the little creatures, leaning against the tree and putting her cheek against it. But the warmth was only faint, and all around them the wind still howled.

Miranda took off her skis. "We're protected from the storm here, but it's still frightfully cold."

Charlie nodded. She was worried

about her father, all the way up on
the mountaintop. She tried contacting
Random on her mini-com again, but all
she heard was static.

"Help me with this," Miranda called.
Charlie turned and saw her struggling
with a fallen bough. Together they lifted
it, propping it against the trunk of the tree.
The snowpops watched with fascination.

"Now that one," said Miranda, pointing
to another log. "Lean it next to the first.
We'll try to make a shelter."

They propped the boughs together and
added two more. The snowpops scampered
off, returning with fistfuls of smaller
branches that they dragged along the
ground.

Miranda couldn't help smiling. "Thank
you," she said, weaving the branches into
the shelter to create a screen against the
wind.

"Not bad at all," Charlie said. "How did you learn to do that?"

"My father taught me," said Miranda. "We go on a lot of expeditions together, out into the woods or sailing to different islands. He says it's important to know how to survive, if disaster strikes."

Charlie heard the admiration in Miranda's voice.

"Well, disaster definitely struck this time," Charlie chuckled.

They huddled inside the shelter, wrapping their jackets around them. The branches kept out the worst of the wind, and the tree trunk at their backs offered a hint of warmth. But it was still shiveringly cold.

Zig-Zag jumped up, scuffling at Charlie's coat. "One second," she said, undoing the zip. The snowpop clambered inside and snuggled down cosily.

Tufty looked nervously up at Miranda, then he hopped into her lap. She shook her head ruefully. "All right," she said, and unzipped her jacket. The little creature scrambled in, letting out a happy purr.

"It actually feels quite nice," Miranda said with a blush. "I shouldn't have behaved so horribly to them. They just surprised me earlier."

"I know," Charlie said. "You could've got really hurt if Random hadn't been there."

Miranda sighed. "I should've been nicer to him too."

Charlie smiled. "He'll be very impressed when I tell him about this shelter. He was originally a constructor droid, after all."

Miranda blushed again. "It's nothing special," she said. Then she frowned. "Is it me, or is it sort of light in here?"

She was right. Charlie could make out

Miranda's face quite clearly, even in the gloom.

"I think it's the tree," she said, turning to touch the bark. There were fine cracks in it, and from some of them a faint

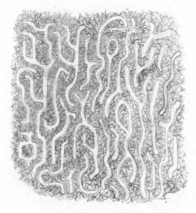

golden light broke through. "I'll have to tell my dad about this, he'll— What is it?"

Zig-Zag was scratching at her collar. His ears were pricked up. Tufty popped his head out of Miranda's coat, his blue eyes bright and alert.

Charlie listened. The wind whistled through the trees but she could hear another sound too. Animals calling, echoing and distant.

"It's the other snowpops!" she said.

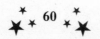

"They must be looking for these two."

Zig-Zag jumped free of her jacket, running to the shelter's opening. But before he reached it, he turned back, taking hold of Charlie's sleeve.

"You want us to go with you," she said.

Miranda wrinkled her nose. "They're animals, Charlie. We don't even know if the big ones are friendly. We should stay here, where it's safe."

Charlie bit her lip. "Look, this shelter's great," she said. "Really. But the temperature is already well below freezing and soon it'll be dark. We need help."

"But how will following these two help?" Miranda asked. "We could end up stuck in the snow while they curl up in some nice warm burrow that we can't even fit into."

"I know it's a risk," Charlie said, "but I don't think these snowpops are as silly as they seem. In fact, I think they're quite smart. And they wouldn't ask us to go with them if they didn't think it would help."

Zig-Zag crouched in the doorway, looking back at Charlie. The howl sounded again, and Tufty let out an expectant whine.

"We should trust them," Charlie told Miranda firmly. "I don't think we have a choice."

## Chapter Six
# Teardrop

Charlie and Miranda followed the snowpops out into the forest. The great plants creaked and groaned in the wind and the shadows were so deep it felt like midnight, though it was barely three in the afternoon.

But things got much worse when they left the shelter of the trees. Charlie could see the ice-cliff ahead of them, still scarred from the accident that morning.

Walking towards it, they found themselves wading through blowing drifts of snow that reached past Charlie's knees.

She clutched Miranda's hand and tried not to get blown off her feet. Up ahead, Tufty and Zig-Zag skipped easily over the snow on their furry feet.

Then suddenly the snowpops vanished. Charlie rubbed her eyes.

"Where are they?" she shouted over the howling gale. "Zig-Zag! Tufty!"

Miranda looked around. "They left us! I knew this was a bad idea."

Then Charlie heard a squeak and saw Zig-Zag's head popping out of the cliff. It was joined by Tufty. Then both of them vanished again.

"Come on," Charlie said, tugging Miranda forward. They reached the cliff, feeling with their hands as the snow gusted in their eyes. Charlie found an opening, and heard the scrabble of paws inside.

She crouched and pushed her way in, then she reached back to help Miranda. The wind had dropped, and she could look around.

They were in a narrow tunnel, too low to stand up in but just big enough to crawl along. The two snowpops sat a short distance away, chattering to the girls. Then they turned and darted off along the tunnel.

"I suppose we'd better follow them," Miranda said doubtfully.

Charlie nodded. "At least we're out of the storm!"

She crawled along the passage on her hands and knees, glad of her thick trousers and heavy gloves. The tunnel was dark but she could see her way – the walls were made entirely of ice, and from somewhere a pale light came filtering through.

Miranda struggled along behind her, grumbling as her skis scraped on the ceiling. "Stupid things," she muttered. "I should have left them back in the shelter."

"But they're the only ones on Vela!" Charlie reminded her.

Miranda laughed. "Very clever."

Then Charlie heard a squeaking up ahead, and froze. It was the same cry they'd heard from the forest, a long,

echoing call that rose and fell. Zig-Zag and Tufty called back and bounded off excitedly. Charlie followed.

Soon she was aware of a light up ahead, a cosy glow shining through the walls of ice. Suddenly the tunnel opened out to reveal a large, open space.

The floor was circular and dipped slightly in the middle, and overhead the ceiling tapered to a point. The walls were made entirely of ice, shimmering like glass.

# Cosmic Creatures

*It's like being inside a frozen teardrop,* Charlie thought.

The floor of the teardrop had a carpet of earth and moss. In the middle, a plant sprouted, just like the ones outside. Its branches spread out to cover the sides of the teardrop, all linked together like a web.

But that wasn't the most remarkable thing. All the way up the tree trunk, lines of bark had been stripped off. From these stripes, a friendly golden glow filled every corner of the space. Charlie could feel warmth on her face too, radiating from the plant.

"Wow," she said. "Now my dad's *really* going to get excited."

Zig-Zag and Tufty raced forward, letting out excited squeaks. Charlie heard a rustling overhead and looked up to see a face peering down at them through the

branches. It was large and furry, and its eyes were soft and friendly.

The snowpop unfolded itself, climbing down from what Charlie realised was a nest of twigs and moss suspended in the branches. Zig-Zag and Tufty scrambled up and the big snowpop purred as they were all reunited.

Then the snowpop swung down towards Charlie and Miranda, landing on two feet. It barely came up to Charlie's waist, but Miranda still took a nervous step back.

"It's OK," Charlie whispered, "it's their dad. I don't think he's going to hurt us."

The snowpop padded towards them, his long arms almost scraping the floor.

"Um, hello," Charlie said, putting out a hand. "It's nice to meet you."

The creature sniffed the air. He let out a grumbling growl.

Then Charlie felt something on her
shoulder and looked round in surprise.
Zig-Zag had dropped from the tree on
to her jacket, waving both hands and
chattering. Tufty dropped on to Miranda's
head, then he clambered into her arms.
She smiled and stroked his fur.

Their father scratched his head.
Then he reached up into the branches,
tugging something loose. He reached out,

extending a paw to Charlie. In it was a large, oddly shaped brown fruit.

She took it. It smelled like damp wood. The creature looked at her expectantly so Charlie slowly took a bite, forcing herself to smile. The taste was even worse than the smell – like a cross between rotting mushrooms and mouldy bread.

"Thank you very much," she told the snowpop. Then she held out the fruit to Miranda. "Here, eat some. We don't want to offend them."

Miranda shot Charlie a look but took a bite. "Thank you," she muttered. "How nice."

## Chapter Seven
# The Ice Warren

There was a sudden crackling sound
and the daddy snowpop jumped. Charlie
reached into her pocket. Her mini-com
was receiving a signal.

"Random?" she spoke into it. "Random,
can you hear me? Dad, is that you?"

The static hissed, and for a moment she
thought she could almost hear a voice.
Then the signal went dead again.

Charlie groaned. "What if they were

calling for help?"

"What can we do?" said Miranda. "They're all the way up there, and we're stuck down here."

Charlie turned to the daddy snowpop. "It's our dads," she said. "They tried to climb the mountain, and... Oh, this is no good."

The creature was staring at her, baffled. But Zig-Zag, crouched on her shoulder, seemed to understand. He turned to his dad, chattering and waving his arms. The big snowpop listened, then his eyes lit up.

He looked up at the ceiling, then back at Charlie. Then he beckoned for her to follow.

"I think he understood," Charlie said to Miranda.

"Or he's just trying to be polite," she muttered.

The snowpop led them to another low

74

tunnel on the far side of the teardrop. Tufty bounded after him, and Zig-Zag reached up to tug on Charlie's sleeve.

Charlie and Miranda crawled after the snowpops. Soon they came to a larger passage, and Charlie found that she could stand up. On either side she saw openings and tunnels, and more of those teardrop-shaped chambers with glowing plants in the centre. Many were occupied by families of snowpops, swinging from the branches or feasting on the strange fruit while the little ones rolled on the floor.

"I wonder how many of them there are in here," Miranda whispered.

"I don't know," Charlie said. "But this glacier must be pretty huge. I'm really glad your dad didn't keep on climbing. Who knows how much damage he could've done."

Miranda didn't reply.

Soon they came to a larger chamber, and Charlie heard Miranda gasp. It was the same teardrop shape as the others but this space was huge, as high as the tallest building in First Landing, and the same distance across. Again, there was a vast tree growing in its centre, its branches rising high above them.

Zig-Zag led them to the tree's massive trunk, and Charlie felt its light and warmth on her face. Sections of the bark had been peeled away to leave a dark ribbon running all the way up the tree, winding round the trunk like a half-peeled apple.

Zig-Zag ran forward and balanced on the bark. He used it to scamper up the tree. "It's a kind of walkway," Charlie realised, stepping up on to the ribbon of bark and using the trunk of the tree to

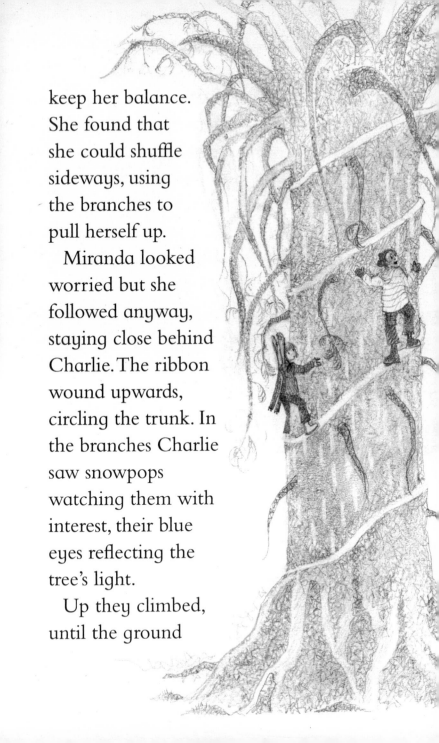

keep her balance.
She found that
she could shuffle
sideways, using
the branches to
pull herself up.

Miranda looked
worried but she
followed anyway,
staying close behind
Charlie. The ribbon
wound upwards,
circling the trunk. In
the branches Charlie
saw snowpops
watching them with
interest, their blue
eyes reflecting the
tree's light.

Up they climbed,
until the ground

below was hidden by the branches and
all Charlie could see was the grey boughs
and green fronds. The air seemed much
thinner here, and after the long climb
Charlie felt short of breath.

Soon the branches thinned out, and she
realised that they'd almost reached the
ceiling. A long branch formed a bridge
to the cavern wall, leading to another
narrow tunnel. They followed it, winding
deeper into the ice. Then the daddy
snowpop paused and pointed. Miranda let
out a groan.

Ahead of them was another tunnel
leading upwards and, far away, Charlie
could hear the distant howl of the wind.
But the tunnel was very steep, like a
chimney leading straight up to the
surface.

Tufty clambered up, pursued by his
brother. The daddy snowpop looked at

Charlie, nodding his head towards the surface.

"We'll be right behind you," she said.

She started climbing up, finding small fingerholds and footholds in the ice. It was tricky – the walls were slippery and smooth – but she was just able to pull herself up. Miranda followed, straining and muttering.

Then Charlie heard a scraping crash and looked back.
Miranda had missed her footing and slid back down the chimney. It wasn't far, but she'd landed hard. She groaned,

shaking off her backpack and skis.

"Stupid things," she said. "I'll leave them here. That'll make it easier."

She grabbed for a handhold and started to pull herself back up. But Charlie could see the strain on her face.

"It's not far," she said encouragingly. "Then hopefully we'll find our dads and get out of here."

Miranda opened her mouth to say something, but just then she lost her grip again and slid back to the bottom, landing on her backpack.

"I can't do it!" she cried, jumping up and kicking the wall in frustration. Charlie saw tears on her cheeks. "I can't climb up there. I'm useless."

"You're not useless," Charlie said, clinging on. "You built the shelter, and you saved us with those skis. Maybe you're just not a climber."

Miranda sighed. "The truth is, I hate it.

I hate heights, and I hate ropes, and I hate cold. I just hate it." She looked at Charlie. "Don't tell my dad, OK? Promise me."

"I promise," Charlie said. "But look, you don't have to like everything he likes. And you don't have to be good at everything either. My mum loves fixing things, but if I try to help, I make a total mess. We all have different stuff we're good at. Even your dad, I bet."

Miranda frowned, like she'd never thought of this before.

"And you don't have to climb up," Charlie went on. "I'll find them and come back for you. Just stay there. I won't be long."

## Chapter Eight
# The Ledge

A wall of wind hit Charlie as she clambered from the ice chimney. She could see nothing – the sky was deep black and when she pulled out her mini-com and activated the built-in torch, all she saw was snow.

Zig-Zag and Tufty were waiting by the opening and as soon as Charlie climbed out they jumped on her, burying themselves in the warmth of her jacket.

Their father crouched nearby, as though waiting for something.

Then a shape appeared. It was another snowpop, taller than the others with grey, snow-covered fur. She chattered, and Zig-Zag and Tufty's father chattered back. Then the grey snowpop lumbered away. Zig-Zag tugged on Charlie's coat.

"Got it," she said. "We need to follow her."

Within a few steps Charlie felt completely lost. She had no idea how high up the mountain they were, or which way they were facing, or whether she was about to walk off a cliff.

# Cosmic Creatures

Charlie kept her torch on, lighting up the grey snowpop, who shuffled ahead through the snow, leading them steadily uphill.

At last the snowpop paused and pointed. They had reached the shelter of a tall rock, which protected them from the worst of the wind. Charlie shone her torch ahead, and immediately wished she hadn't.

On one side the rocky cliff rose, sturdy and strong. But on the other the ground fell away, and beyond it was nothing but darkness. A narrow ledge of rock stuck out from the cliff, and it was towards this that the snowpop was pointing. She took shuffling steps, and Charlie took a deep breath and followed her.

She clung to the cliff as the wind drove at her. The narrow ledge was slippery underfoot. "I don't think this is a very good idea," Charlie told Zig-Zag and Tufty, who were wriggling inside her jacket. "But the ledge gets wider soon and we're nearly—"

She lost her footing, the ledge cracked and she tumbled over the edge.

Charlie dropped into the darkness, clutching the snowpops tight against her. She just had time to let out a startled shout when she realised she wasn't falling any more.

She was floating. And she could feel something – a familiar tingling all around her.

"Random!" she cried out happily, as beams of light fell across her face.

The robot floated into view, his golden eyes shining like torches, his whole body rocking as gusts of wind pummelled him. With a hum of effort, he lifted Charlie back up to the wide ledge where the two adult snowpops were waiting.

"I picked you up on my sensors," said Random, as Charlie found her feet. "At first I thought it was another of your furry friends, then I realised it was too large."

In the glow from his golden eyes Charlie saw movement behind the two snowpops, and her heart leapt.

"Dad!" she cried as Kwame emerged from behind a rock. He looked frozen and windswept, but he grinned with relief as he ran to Charlie and clasped her in a shivering hug.

"I don't believe it," Kwame said. "Random told us he'd detected something nearby, but I never dreamed it could be you."

The captain emerged from the shelter of the rocks, looking rather damp and sorry for himself. "Where is Miranda?" he asked.

"She's safe,"' Charlie told him. "We'll go back to her, and I'll explain everything on the way."

The captain hesitated, looking regretfully over his shoulder. "But we were so close," he said. "We were nearly at the top when the storm came."

Kwame put a hand on his arm. "You'll be back," he said.

## Chapter Nine
# Snowfoot

They found Miranda waiting at the
bottom of the ice chimney, sitting on her
backpack and looking glum. Kwame had
secured a rope at the top of the shaft, and
that made the climb down much easier.

Charlie slid her way to the bottom, glad
to be out of the howling wind. Zig-Zag
and Tufty scampered after her, followed
by their father and the old, grey snowpop.

Miranda got to her feet as her father

emerged from the tunnel. The captain looked weary and defeated, his shoulders slumped. Miranda ran over and hugged him.

"The mountain has beaten me," he said. "But I'm glad you're safe."

"You tried your best," Miranda told him. "And we'll try again."

The captain held her at arm's length. "I must apologise to you," he said. "I was so focused on getting to the top that I didn't think about the risks, either to myself or to you, my precious daughter. From what Charlie tells me, your quick thinking saved you both."

Miranda blushed. "I only did what you taught me. Build a shelter, try to stay warm."

"She was brilliant," Charlie said.

"I'm proud of you," said the captain. "I'm sorry I put you in danger."

Miranda opened her mouth nervously, then she shut it again. Charlie reached out and squeezed her arm. "Go on," she said. "Tell him."

"It's not just your fault," Miranda blurted out. "The truth is, I wasn't ready for this expedition. I haven't done enough climbing, and I don't … I don't want to…"

The captain's face softened. "You can tell me, whatever it is."

"I'm scared," Miranda admitted. "I'm scared of heights. My head goes all fuzzy and my heart beats fast and I can't think straight. You know I'm not scared of most things, but I *just hate heights*."

"Why didn't you say this before?" the captain asked. "I would never have asked you to come."

"I didn't want you to be disappointed." Miranda sighed. "I knew how much you

wanted to climb the mountain and name it after yourself."

The captain blushed. "It all sounds a bit silly now, doesn't it? After we've all risked our lives for my stupid pride."

"It wasn't stupid," Miranda insisted. "It was brave."

The captain smiled. "Maybe it was a bit of both. But either way, I don't think I deserve to name this mountain after myself. How about I name it after you instead? Mount Miranda has a nice ring to it."

Miranda shook her head. "You can't name a mountain after someone who's scared of heights. But I've got a better idea. We should name it after the real heroes of today."

The captain looked at Random. "You can't possibly mean the robot?"

Miranda laughed. "I do like the name

Mount Random," she said. "But I mean our new friends. It's their mountain, after all."

She gestured to the snowpops, who hopped up and down and squeaked excitedly.

The captain narrowed his eyes. "What are their names?"

"I call them Zig-Zag and Tufty," Charlie put in. "But I've named the species snowpops."

The captain frowned again. "Mount Snowpop is bad. Mount Tufty is even worse!" he said. "Are you absolutely sure about that name – snowpop? It might suit the little ones, but these grown-ups are proud creatures. Noble, and wise."

He gestured to the snowpop father and his grey companion. Charlie realised he was right. The name didn't suit them at all.

"Back where I come from on Earth,"
Kwame said, "in the mountains of North
America, there's the legend of a creature
called Bigfoot. It's said to be furry and
walk upright, not too different from these
creatures here."

"But they're not big," Miranda pointed out. "So the name doesn't fit."

"So how about Snowfoot?" Charlie suggested. "A bit of my name for them, and a bit of Dad's?"

Captain Robertson nodded approvingly. "I like it. And Mount Snowfoot is a fine name. It lets everyone know who this great peak truly belongs to."

"I can't wait for you to see the rest of their home," Charlie told her dad. "They've got these massive plants and they glow and everything, it's amazing.'

Kwame's eyes shone. "I'm looking forward to it," he said. "But most of all I'm just glad you're OK."

"Well, me too," Charlie said. "I'm glad Random kept an eye on you."

The robot let out a purring hum. "Your family are my responsibility," he said. "Every one of them."

Zig-Zag hopped up on Charlie's shoulder, nuzzling against her face. Then he tugged open her coat and scrambled inside, snuggling up in the warmth.

Miranda gave a squeak of surprise as she felt Tufty doing the same, climbing her leg like a tree trunk then crawling inside her jacket. His big eyes and pointed ears popped out of the top, and Miranda giggled.

"All right, little friend," she said. "You can stay there for now."

Look out for another adventure
with Charlie and Random:

## Chapter One
# The Shimmering Pools

Charlie floated happily on her back, held up by the warm water. Thin clouds of steam swirled over her head, allowing shafts of sunlight to sparkle on the water's surface.

That was how the Shimmering Pools got their name, and it made them one of the most beautiful places Charlie knew. There were deep pools and shallow pools, waterfalls and streams, all heated by springs that flowed from deep caves in the mountainside. They were the perfect temperature for bathing. On a hot day the water seemed cool and refreshing, while on a chilly day like this one it made you feel warm and relaxed.

"It's so lovely, you should come in," Charlie said, peering up at her little brother, Maki. He sat perched on the bank, wrapped in his fleece jacket.

But Maki shook his head. "I don't feel like it. Besides, I want to finish this game." He looked back down at the silver tablet propped on his knees. He tapped buttons and the game let out high-pitched *beep-bloop* noises.

Charlie knew that Maki wasn't really telling the whole truth. He wasn't afraid of the water, exactly – he was fine in the town baths, where all the children of First Landing learned to swim. He just didn't like the Shimmering Pools.

She wondered if it was because there were fish in here – little shoals of silver sprats and large, purple catfish with long dark whiskers. Or perhaps it was the slippery green algae on the rocks all around that put him off. Either way, Charlie wasn't going to push if her brother didn't feel brave enough.

"I'm hungry," Maki said, putting the game down at last. "Is it time for our sandwiches yet?"

Charlie stood, and found her balance

on the slippery rocks. "It must be," she said, "because I'm hungry too."

She waded to the bank and clambered up, shivering as she wrapped herself in a towel. From up here she could see right down the mountain slope to First Landing, a dark jumble of buildings spread out beneath the clear, cold sky.

The town was the first human colony on planet Vela. It had been founded by Charlie's parents and their fellow settlers from Earth, who had come here to study the local plants and wildlife and to build a new home in balance with nature.

But the streets of the town seemed unusually quiet today. Normally they would be packed with vehicles, from small one-person transporters to huge electric haulers carrying building materials. Instead, every person she could see was on foot, and they were all bundled up in layers of clothing.

Charlie knew why straight away. They'd been having problems with First Landing's power supply for weeks, which meant that no one could charge up their vehicles, heat their water or run their radiators. And now the weather had turned cooler, it was making things rather uncomfortable.

The power shortages had even affected Charlie's robot friend, Random. She could see him just along the bank, his rounded steel body resting beneath a gold-leafed tree, his systems shut down to save energy. She hoped they could find a new power source soon – these "naps" of his were getting longer and longer.

"So, what did Dad put in the sandwiches?" Charlie asked, pulling on her jacket and turning towards Maki. "I hope it's not that nasty fish paste ag—"

She broke off in surprise as something soared through the steam. She didn't see it clearly. It was just a shadow, darting past Maki then vanishing again.

Her brother didn't notice, he was too busy investigating their packed lunch. But he looked up at Charlie as she rubbed her eyes and blinked.

"Are you OK?" he asked.

Charlie frowned. "Yes, I just thought… Never mind. Pass me a sandwich."